THE INVISIBLE SWORD

VISHNU SIRIPURAM

To all the fiction lovers and readers,
the dreamers, the night thinkers,
the ones who believe in magic even when the world
doesn't.

This story is for you.
May you always find a sword to carry,
a battle worth fighting,
and a story that makes you feel seen.

Contents

Contents

Foreword

Every once in a while, a story comes along that blends myth with emotion, fantasy with struggle, and legend with the raw experience of being human. Invisible Sword is one such tale.

At its core, this is the journey of Arnav, a young man who begins as a nobody, lost in the shadows of a world that never sees him. But through a series of surreal events, he is thrust into a hidden war between ancient powers, given a destiny he never asked for, and handed a sword born of a dragon's soul. What follows is not just a battle against evil, but a deeper confrontation with self-doubt, responsibility, and the choices that define a hero.

This isn't a story of perfection. Arnav stumbles, makes terrible mistakes, and pays dearly for them. And yet, that's what makes his story unforgettable because it mirrors our own struggles in the face of power, pain, and purpose.

Invisible Sword is more than a fantasy thriller. It's a meditation on power and consequence, on identity and redemption. Whether you're a fan of ancient legends, epic battles, or simply tales of growth and inner conflict, Arnav's journey will leave a mark on your heart.

So open these pages and follow the path through darkness, mystery, and fate to discover what it truly means to be chosen.

Preface

Invisible Sword was born from a single question: What if the greatest battles we fight are the ones within ourselves?

As I began writing this story, I didn't set out to create a hero. I set out to create a human being flawed, uncertain, often afraid. Arnav, the protagonist of this tale, is not the chosen one in the traditional sense. He's not gifted with charm, strength, or popularity. He's someone who's been ignored, laughed at, even broken. And yet, when fate places a legendary weapon in his hands, his life changes not because he becomes powerful, but because he is forced to confront who he truly is.

This story weaves fantasy with reality. There are glowing caves and ancient monks, invisible swords and forgotten kingdoms. But beneath all that magic lies something deeply human: the fear of failure, the desire to belong, the pain of making the wrong choice and the courage to try again anyway.

Every chapter reflects a part of the journey we all go through searching for meaning, facing demons (both real and metaphorical), and learning what it truly means to be strong. Through Arnav's struggles and victories, I hope you'll find echoes of your own story.

This book is not just about a boy who becomes a warrior. It's about how every broken soul still carries the spark of greatness if they're brave enough to wield it.

Thank you for stepping into this world. I hope it challenges you, moves you, and above all, stays with you.

Acknowledgements

Writing The Invisible Sword has been one of the most transformative journeys of my life, and it would not have been possible without the love, support, and belief of those around me.

To my family — thank you for always standing by me, even when I disappeared into my world of dragons, swords, and ancient kings. Your patience and encouragement have meant everything.

To my friends — your constant check-ins, pep talks, and late-night story discussions gave me the strength to keep going.

And a special shout-out to Faizan, Varshini, and Sharat, thank you for believing in this story even before I believed in myself. You were the real light in the dark moments of doubt. This book carries pieces of your energy on every page.

This story is for all of you
because every hero's journey is built on the shoulders of those who never let them fall.

With love,
VISHNU

Prologue

Somewhere, in a time before time...

Long before cities rose and empires crumbled, before machines hummed and men forgot the language of stars — there was a war.

A war not fought for land, but for power buried deep beneath the earth — a power born of fire, sealed by sacrifice, and guarded by a blade forged from a dragon's soul.

The warrior who once wielded that sword was not born ordinary. And when he died, the world changed.

The sword did not.

It slept — waiting. Waiting for the return of a soul born under the same stars, carrying the same fire in his veins. A soul that would awaken not in palaces or temples, but in the unnoticed corners of the modern world... quiet, overlooked, invisible.

But destiny never forgets.

And the sword is ready to be found again.

CHAPTER ONE

THE ESCAPE

Arnav came from the kind of home where silence wasn't awkward, it was just normal.

Their two-bedroom apartment sat in the middle of a sleepy lane surrounded by small shops and peeling posters. His father, Suresh Sharma, was a factory supervisor serious, disciplined, and always on schedule. He left home each morning by 7 a.m., his lunchbox packed with quiet precision. His mother, Meena, was a housewife with soft hands and tired eyes, always humming old songs as she chopped vegetables. Their life wasn't full of luxuries, but it wasn't unhappy. They had enough to get by no frills, no vacations, no complaints.

Love in their home was quiet. It was in the way his father checked the water tank before leaving. It was in the way his mother folded his clothes and kept them near his bed, even though he rarely thanked her.

Arnav, however, always felt slightly out of place.

From the time he was a child, he was different. He wasn't the boy who ran out to play cricket in the lane, or who asked for toys during Diwali. He kept to himself—rarely spoke more than a few words unless spoken to. His emotions stayed tucked away, like unused notebooks. Even at home, he wasn't one to share how his day had gone or what bothered him. His parents didn't push. They just quietly accepted that he was... quiet.

He was short for his age, something he had learned to live with. While other boys had grown taller and broader through high school, Arnav had remained thin and undersized, with narrow shoulders and legs that looked too fragile to run. He hated group photos. He hated being called "chhotu" by strangers. He especially hated being asked if he was in the wrong class on the first day of college.

But he never said anything. He simply smiled politely, faintly and moved on.

College wasn't much better than school. The cliques had changed, but the rules hadn't. If you weren't loud, athletic, confident, or cool, you were invisible. And being invisible came with its own dangers.

That morning was cloudy, the air humid. Arnav reached college with his usual slouch, bag hanging from one shoulder, headphones in but no music playing. He walked past the familiar graffiti on the walls, past the chai vendor who never remembered his order, past the kids who always seemed to be laughing at something.

When he entered the classroom, it was already buzzing. Laughter, banter, the shuffling of chairs. He slipped into a back bench, eyes down, heart quiet.

His shoes felt strange but he didn't think much of it.

"Arnav Sharma," the professor called during roll call, barely glancing up from the register.

Arnav stood.

And immediately fell.

His feet caught mid-step, tangled in something. The floor rushed up to meet him. He landed hard, elbows scraping against the tiles, chin smacking down. His notebook flew from his hands, pages fluttering like broken wings. The class paused.

And then—laughter. Loud, vicious, echoing through the room like applause after a bad play.

Someone pointed at his shoes, doubled over with laughter. "Bhai, who tied your laces together? Kindergarten prank, bro!"

Arnav sat up slowly, heat rising in his cheeks. He looked down.

His shoelaces were knotted tightly double-knotted, actually. Someone had done it while he wasn't paying attention.

The laughter didn't stop. If anything, it grew. Even the professor tried to hide a smirk before mumbling something about "settling down." But no one helped. No one reached out a hand. No one asked if he was okay.

He wasn't okay.

He didn't say a word. He just got up, gathered his things, and walked out.

The laughter followed him like a shadow, sticking to the back of his neck.

Outside, the sky threatened rain. He kept walking. Past the gates, past the cycle stand, past the street dogs sleeping in the shade. He didn't care where he was going. He just needed to go.

His legs carried him through familiar lanes and unfamiliar turns. Somewhere between the auto stand and a row of rundown godowns, he started to run.

He didn't run often. His thin legs weren't built for it. But that day, his body moved like it needed to escape itself.

He ran until the noise of the city began to fade.

He found himself near the edge of town, in a place he didn't recognize. The buildings were older here, walls covered in green moss, the ground soft with damp earth. Two massive banyan trees framed a narrow trail, half-hidden behind overgrown bushes. At the entrance stood a rusted gate, slightly ajar, creaking with the breeze.

Something about it called to him.

He stepped through.

The trail twisted and dipped, uneven and slippery. He walked slowly now, heart still pounding, shirt sticking to his back. The air smelled of rain-soaked roots and something ancient. The wind whispered like it carried stories.

And then his foot slipped.

A rock, hidden beneath leaves.

His arms flailed. His body twisted. The world spun.

He tumbled down the slope branches scratching his skin, mud staining his clothes, pain flaring in his side. It felt like forever before he landed, breathless, at the bottom.

For a few moments, he lay still.

Eyes wide open, staring at the canopy of tangled trees above.

Everything hurt his wrist, his back, his pride. But the silence was thick, comforting. No voices. No laughter. Just his breath, the chirp of hidden birds, and the distant rustle of leaves.

He exhaled slowly.

For the first time in years, he felt far away from all the places that had made him feel small.

And for the first time... it felt good.

CHAPTER TWO

THE HIDDEN PATH

Arnav's body ached. His shirt clung to his skin, streaked with dirt and leaves. A small cut on his arm stung as sweat ran into it, but he barely noticed. He sat up slowly, blinking away the dizziness, and took in his surroundings.

He was in a forest dense and wild.

Thick trees towered over-head, their branches so tightly woven that the sky above was barely visible. Moss crept along the trunks, and the ground was littered with damp leaves, rocks, and thick roots that jutted out like the bones of the earth itself. The air was cool, filled with the smell of wet bark and something older... something strangely metallic.

He had never seen this place before. And yet, it felt like it had been waiting for him.

"Where... am I?" he whispered to himself, his voice barely audibles against the forest's hush.

He stood, wobbling a little, brushing off his jeans. His phone had no signal not even a flicker of network. Not that he expected one. This place felt like it belonged outside of time.

He took a cautious step forward.

That's when he saw it.

Nestled beneath an ancient tree with twisted roots was a hole. Not just any hole it was circular, wide enough for a person to crawl into, and surrounded by strange markings etched into the earth like runes. The roots curled around it like gnarled fingers, protecting its secret.

From deep within the hole, a soft glow pulsed. Dim, but steady. It throbbed gently, like a heartbeat.

Arnav froze.

Every part of him screamed to turn back. To climb up the slope and pretend this never happened. But another part deeper, older whispered something else.

Go.

He knelt beside the hole, peering into the glow. The path inside seemed to slope downward, almost like a tunnel. Cool air rose from within, carrying the faint scent of smoke... or was it incense?

He didn't know why, but he reached out his hand. His fingers brushed the edge of the glowing ring and suddenly, he felt it.

A pulse. Like a spark running up his arm.

He jerked back, heart thudding.

Was he imagining it?

He looked around. The forest was quiet, watching.

He took a breath.

And then without really thinking, he slid into the tunnel.

The earth swallowed him instantly.

The passage was steep. The ground slipped under his shoes, and gravity took over. He tumbled again arms flailing, dirt flying. The world narrowed into spinning earth and shadow.

He didn't fall far this time, but when he landed, the world around him had changed.

He was in a cavern.

Wide and open, the air still but charged. The stone walls glistened faintly, as if painted with light. Glowing stones—blue, violet, and white were embedded all around, their glow reflecting in ripples across the damp floor.

It was beautiful. And terrifying.

As Arnav stood, brushing soil from his palms, he heard a sound—soft footsteps echoing off the cavern walls.

And then, out of the shadows, came a figure.

A man.

Tall. Motionless. Dressed in flowing robes that seemed to shift in colour as they moved, like clouds at dusk. His head was shaved, and his skin was ageless. He wore no expression yet his eyes...

His eyes were ancient.

"You have arrived," the man said, his voice calm, deep, and without surprise.

Arnav's mouth went dry. "Who... who are you?"

The man gave a faint smile. "A guide. Nothing more."

Arnav shook his head. "What is this place? What's happening to me?"

"You found what many ignore," the monk said. "Pain led you here. But now... pain must shape you."

Arnav took a step back. "I didn't come here for anything. I was just—"

"Running," the monk finished for him. "From them. From yourself."

Arnav swallowed hard. "What do you want?"

The monk's eyes darkened slightly. "It's not about what I want. It's about what you are meant to become."

There was a long pause. The cavern hummed.

"You must prove yourself," the monk said finally.

"How?"

The monk's tone shifted, firmer now. "You must face evil... and destroy it."

Arnav blinked. "Destroy?"

"You must kill a man," the monk said, without hesitation. "A criminal. One whose hands are soaked in blood."

Arnav's stomach dropped. "Kill? You want me to *kill* someone?"

"Only by confronting true darkness," the monk said, "can you uncover your own."

Arnav felt like the ground was slipping beneath him again.

"This is insane," he whispered. "I'm just a student—I'm not—"

"Special?" the monk offered gently. "Chosen? Brave?"

Arnav couldn't answer.

"You came here unloved, unheard, invisible," the monk continued. "But your fate is not to remain so."

He turned, slowly disappearing into the shadows.

"Wait!" Arnav called after him. "Why me? Why now?"

But there was no reply.

Suddenly, the walls trembled—just for a moment. A low rumble shook the cavern floor. Lights flickered in the stones, and a wind seemed to pass through the underground chamber.

Before Arnav could move or call out again—

Everything vanished.

CHAPTER THREE

THE RETURN TO SILENCE

Arnav's mind spun as he stumbled, gasping for air. The cavern, the monk's cryptic words, the glowing stones, they were all fading into something distant, unreal, as if they had never existed at all. His body still trembled from the encounter, the weight of what he had just experienced pressing down on him. But when he opened his eyes, everything was different.

The cavern's cool stone walls vanished, replaced by the familiar concrete of the college storeroom. The warm, damp air of the underground space was gone, replaced by the dry, stifling heat of the room. He blinked several times, trying to process it, but the buzzing fluorescent lights overhead did nothing to clear the fog in his mind.

The hum of voices from outside the room drifted in, the distant chatter of students walking through the halls. It was as if the cavern had never existed, as if he had only dreamt it. But... that couldn't be true. He had *felt* it. The monk's words still echoed in his mind. *"You must face evil... and destroy it."*

He shook his head, trying to clear the confusion.

His legs felt unsteady as he rose, a familiar ache in his bones but not the kind of pain he had experienced in the cave. There had been scratches on his arms, cuts and bruises from his fall, the sting of his wrist, the throb in his side. The memories of those sensations should have been fresh. But now, there was nothing.

Nothing.

He looked down at his clothes, his shirt stained with mud; his jeans still torn in places but there were no signs of the wounds he'd suffered in the cave. No marks, no blood, no discomfort. His wrist should have been swollen, his back should have been sore, his side still throbbing. Yet there was nothing. He twisted his wrist experimentally, then ran his fingers across the back of his neck. It was as if the cave had never touched him.

"Was it a dream?" he whispered to himself, his voice barely audibles in the empty room.

The thought gnawed at him. But as his eyes wandered, something caught his attention a faint rustling, a soft breeze that didn't belong in a sealed, dusty storeroom.

The paper.

It appeared from the corner of the room, fluttering gently in the air, as if carried by an invisible hand. It drifted toward him, slow and deliberate. Arnav reached out, instinctively catching it, the paper light as air.

He looked at the words written on it.

"I'm waiting for you."

The message felt too deliberate, too precise, to be nothing. But then, a cold wave of realization passed over him. It was just a scrap of paper.

Nothing important.

Arnav dropped it, letting it fall to the floor, crumpled at his feet. It was only paper nothing more. Just another insignificant piece of detritus in this forgotten corner of the storeroom. His heart beat faster, but it wasn't from fear or anxiety; it was the rush of frustration, of confusion. Why did this feel like it meant something when it was just a trick? Just a paper caught in a draft.

He turned and walked away, pushing open the creaky door to the hallway. The noise of students laughing, talking, filled the space around him. The world had resumed its normal rhythm, as if nothing had happened.

Yet, as he stepped out into the familiar corridor, something shifted deep inside him. The cavern, the monk, the message none of it felt like it was finished. The world he had just returned to didn't feel real.

And a cold, unsettling thought crept into his mind:

It was waiting for him, somewhere, just beyond the edge of his understanding.

CHAPTER FOUR

ECHOES

The rest of the day passed like a fogged-up mirror-blurry, distant, and quiet.

After leaving the storeroom, Arnav wandered the campus for a while, unsure whether to question what had happened or just forget it entirely. He didn't talk to anyone. Not that anyone noticed. He kept his head low, drifted through his classes, and when the final bell rang, he walked back home like he always did his bag pulling down one shoulder, his mind somewhere else entirely.

At home, everything felt normal. Almost too normal.

His mother greeted him with the usual, "Wash your hands and come eat." The living room smelled of turmeric and fried mustard seeds. His father sat at the dining table with his glasses perched low on his nose, scribbling something in his old black ledger. The TV was on, humming gently in the background.

Dinner came and went. The same dal. The same silence.

That night, after shutting his books with no real interest in them, Arnav stepped out of his room and headed toward the living room. The lights were dim. His father was on the sofa, half-reclined, remote in hand, watching the evening news with his usual stern focus.

"Papa," Arnav said, "can we change the channel?"

His father didn't even look at him. "It's the news. Go watch in your room."

Arnav sighed and sat on the floor, pulling a cushion to his chest. His eyes settled on the screen without really watching until something jolted him upright.

The reporter's face was calm, speaking in a flat, newsreader tone.

But the words...

"I'm waiting for you."

Arnav blinked. *What?*

He turned to his father. "Did you hear that? What did he just say?"

His father glanced at him, clearly annoyed. "The economy something-something. What else do they say? Just the same nonsense every day. Go sleep. College tomorrow."

"But... I heard something else."

"Stop imagining things, Arnav."

Arnav looked back at the screen, but the broadcast had moved on. Weather report. Sports highlights. Nothing unusual. Nothing strange.

He didn't argue. He just got up and walked quietly to his room, but something deep in his gut twisted. The same words. Again.

I'm waiting for you.

The next morning arrived with no warning. Arnav hadn't really slept, he'd just drifted in and out, replaying the events in his head. The forest. The cave. The monk. The storeroom. The paper. The television.

It all sat inside him like a knot that wouldn't unravel.

By the time he reached college, a dull ache pulsed behind his eyes. He felt drowsy, disconnected. His body moved, but his mind lagged behind.

Inside the classroom, the usual chatter and noise echoed off the walls. Arnav sat in the second row today, no idea why. Maybe because the back felt too far from reality.

He stared at the board blankly as the teacher began writing in chalk.

And then, there it was again.

The letters on the board swirled, rearranged themselves. They didn't spell out the lesson title anymore. They spelled something else.

I'm waiting for you.

Arnav's breath caught. He blinked hard, leaned forward.

It was still there. The message. Written in the teacher's precise handwriting, but impossible, absurd.

"Arnav!" a sharp voice cracked through the air.

He didn't respond.

"I said, stand up!"

He didn't hear it. All he could hear were those words ringing in his skull, louder, clearer. Like the teacher's voice was dissolving beneath them.

Suddenly—*thwack!*

A chalk piece hit him square in the forehead.

The class laughed.

Arnav jerked upright, eyes wide, reality snapping back like a rubber band. The board now said *Photosynthesis and Its Types.*

Nothing else.

The teacher crossed his arms, looking unimpressed. "Daydreaming in my class, are we?"

"No... I... I just..."

The class snickered again.

The teacher waved a hand. "You can explain when college ends. Meet me in the staff room. And don't be late."

The rest of the day dragged like a slow march. Every tick of the clock felt louder than it should. Arnav barely touched his lunch. His eyes kept drifting to corners, boards, even passing conversations half-expecting those words to appear again.

When the final bell rang, Arnav made his way to the staff room, heart thudding in his chest.

The teacher sat behind a pile of notebooks, flipping through them with a practiced hand. Without looking up, he said, "Sit."

Arnav obeyed.

"You've been distracted lately. I noticed it last week too."

Arnav didn't reply.

The teacher finally looked at him. His eyes weren't angry just disappointed. "So, here's what you'll do. I'm assigning you some extra work. A special assignment. Nothing big just something to keep you focused. I want it on my desk by Friday."

"But..."

"No excuses," the teacher cut him off. "You clearly need structure. I'm giving you a chance. Take it seriously."

Arnav nodded slowly.

Outside the window, the sky had begun to darken with the promise of another storm.

But inside his mind, a different kind of storm was already brewing.

CHAPTER FIVE

THE TEST

The days blurred into routine college, home, assignments, half-sleeping nights, and strange whispers that only Arnav seemed to hear.

But nothing else... happened. No dreams. No monks. No flying papers.

Just silence.

And so, he tried to forget. Tried to believe it was all in his head.

Until his friend Rohit's birthday.

That evening brought a much-needed distraction. They celebrated at a small restaurant just outside the city, all laughter and music and loud cake-smearing rituals. Arnav laughed more that night than he had in weeks.

By the time he waved goodbye and kicked his bike into gear, the air had grown cold and the road nearly deserted. The moon hung like a pale spectator above the sleeping city.

He was halfway through the empty stretch near the base of the hills when someone jumped into his path.

Arnav swerved and braked hard, the tires screeching against the asphalt.

An old man stood trembling in the road, bundled in rags, eyes wide and filled with panic.

"Please... please help me!" the old man gasped, voice cracking with desperation. "I need to get home."

Arnav, still recovering from the shock, parked the bike at the side. "Are you alright? What happened?"

The man wrung his hands, eyes darting around nervously. "My wife... she's in the hospital. I need to go pay her bills. But I think... I think someone's been following me. I can't walk anymore, and it's too cold."

Arnav hesitated.

It was late. He was tired. But something about the man—his fear, his shivering—tugged at him.

After a moment, Arnav nodded. "Alright. Come on. Where do you live?"

The old man pointed weakly. "Behind that hill. There's a small lane that leads to my house."

Arnav helped him onto the back of the bike. The old man's hands were freezing, his grip trembling.

As they started riding toward the hills, Arnav tried to make small talk. "Why were you walking all the way out here alone?"

"I had to... no choice," the old man muttered. "No one else would help. I was trying to take a shortcut through the hill road... but I was followed."

"Don't worry," Arnav said, scanning the quiet road ahead. "We'll get there safely."

But fate had other plans.

Just as they began to ascend the narrow trail cutting around the hill, two shadows darted from the trees. Arnav barely had time to react before a thick boot slammed into his bike.

The engine died. He was flung sideways, hitting the ground with a painful grunt. Dirt filled his mouth.

"Give us the bag, old man!" one of the thieves snarled, already yanking at the man's belongings.

"No!" Arnav shouted, scrambling to his feet. He lunged forward, trying to push them off but one of the attackers punched him square in the ribs. Another kick sent him back down, gasping for air.

His vision blurred, chest throbbing.

The world tilted.

But then his fingers brushed something cold.

A metal rod. Rusted. Heavy.

Arnav gripped it tight, pulled it up with both hands, and swung.

CRACK!

One thief crumpled instantly, the rod connecting with the back of his head. He tumbled, dazed, and rolled down the hill, vanishing into the darkness below.

The other ran.

Silence fell. The old man remained frozen in place.

Arnav panted, adrenaline rushing through his limbs. His hands trembled, not from cold, but from what he'd just done.

He turned slowly to face the old man.

But the old man... wasn't there anymore.

In his place stood the monk.

The same calm eyes. The same white robes. No blood, no wrinkles, just stillness.

"Congratulations, my boy," the monk said, his voice echoing slightly in the quiet night. "You've proven yourself."

Arnav took a shaky step back. "W-What? What's going on?"

"You helped without expecting anything in return. You protected the helpless, even when afraid. Even when you had a choice to walk away."

Arnav's mind spun. "Was this... all a test?"

"Yes," the monk said gently. "And you passed."

"But why? What do you want from me?"

The monk smiled, and for a second, his face seemed to glow faintly. "I've been waiting for you, Arnav. Now, it's time you know what's truly at stake."

Arnav's breath hitched.

The same words. Again.

"I'm waiting for you."

CHAPTER SIX

THE TALE OF THE INVISIBLE SWORD

Arnav stood still, his breath fogging in the cold air, his heart racing. The old man who had just been shivering with worry now stood tall and composed. The frailty had vanished from his posture, replaced by an ageless calm. His eyes gleamed with something more than human. The night felt heavier now, charged with a presence beyond understanding.

The transformation was too perfect, too sudden.

"What... just happened?" Arnav stammered, his body still aching from the fall.

The old man, now in robes that seemed to shimmer faintly in the moonlight, gave him a slow nod. "Congratulations, Arnav. You've proven yourself worthy."

"Worthy? Worthy of what? Who are you?"

"I am Parivrajaka," the man said. "A wandering monk, yes. But more importantly, a guardian of a truth that has been waiting a thousand years to be revealed."

Arnav blinked. "A thousand years?"

Parivrajaka stepped closer, his voice lowering like a chant. "You have questions. Listen carefully. This truth isn't light, it carries the weight of legends."

The wind howled gently through the trees. Arnav swallowed, nodding.

"Long ago," Parivrajaka began, "there was a mighty king. His name was Vikrantha Shura, ruler of the wealthiest dynasty that ever existed on Earth. His kingdom stretched beyond mountains and oceans. He was not only rich in gold and gems but in honour, strength, and wisdom."

Images seemed to form in Arnav's mind golden palaces, banners fluttering above high towers, warriors in gleaming armour. A kingdom of grandeur.

"King Vikrantha was unmatched in battle," the monk continued. "And in one fated competition of might and spirit, he won something far more powerful than land or title. He won the loyalty of a dragon. Not just any dragon—Vyomdraka, a rare descendant of the Vritra species."

Arnav's breath caught. "A dragon?" he echoed.

"Vyomdraka was fierce, loyal, and ancient. He guarded the skies above Vikrantha's kingdom, a creature of flame and storm. But peace never lasts long in the world of men. One day, a demon rose from Pataal—a shadowed realm beneath the earth. His name was Avyaktakala."

Arnav frowned. The name itself made his skin crawl.

"Avyaktakala sought to conquer the Earth," Parivrajaka said gravely. "Not for dominion, but for wealth, power hidden deep within the earth, beneath the very palace of King Vikrantha. A vault of divine treasures passed down since creation."

"The king fought," the monk continued, his tone sharpening. "Vyomdraka fought beside him. But the demon's power was vast. Even the dragon, mighty as he was, began to falter. As hope waned, the king's scholars and witches revealed an ancient prophecy."

Arnav leaned forward instinctively.

"They spoke of a sacred fire ritual Agni Samskara. Through this, Vyomdraka's essence could be forged into a weapon: a sword unlike any other. It would hold the dragon's strength, speed, and invincibility. It would be the key to the vault the only way to protect its contents from falling into evil hands."

"But to do this... the dragon would have to die."

Arnav's mouth went dry. "The king had to kill his own dragon?"

"Yes," Parivrajaka said. "It broke his heart. But he knew the cost of failure. After long days of mourning and prayer, he made a decision. He would arrange the sacred fire."

A hush fell over the hilltop.

Parivrajaka paused, looking at Arnav with solemn eyes.

"That moment... when he accepted the fire, it changed everything. But what followed the making of the sword, the legacy, the prophecy will come in time."

Arnav stood silent, feeling the gravity of what he had just heard.

The night seemed to pulse around them.

CHAPTER SEVEN

THE WAR BEGINS

Smoke curled into the sky as the sacred fire was prepared atop the holy hill. A ring of monks encircled the flame, chanting in ancient tongues that stirred the very air with their cadence. Crimson banners flapped in the chill wind as nobles and commoners alike stood in reverent silence, their gazes fixed on the figure at the center.

King Vikrantha Shura stood tall, adorned in ceremonial armour forged with sacred etchings. His face was carved in solemn calm, but his heart weighed heavy with grief. Above him, Vyomdraka, his faithful dragon and companion in battle, flew one final circle through the heavens.

The beast's roar echoed across the mountains, not in defiance, but in dignity. As the dragon descended, the ground trembled beneath his immense weight. He landed beside the sacred fire, folding his wings with deliberate grace. His fiery eyes locked onto the king's.

There were no words. None were needed.

Vikrantha stepped forward. The gathered scholars and monks bowed as he approached. One of the elder scholars, cloaked in violet and gold, stepped out from the circle and addressed the king.

"Your Majesty," he began, "the ritual is nearly prepared. But before we proceed, there are truths you must know."

The king nodded. "Speak them."

The scholar raised his hands to the firelight. "The sword forged from Vyomdraka's essence will hold powers beyond any mortal weapon,strength, speed, healing, and the rarest gift of all: invisibility. But these powers are bound to you and you alone."

The king's brow furrowed. "What if another should use this sword?"

The monk's voice grew grave. "Then they would wield only a fragment of its strength. To unlock its full potential, they would have to slay you with it."

Vikrantha's eyes narrowed. "A steep price."

Another scholar stepped forward. "This weapon will also serve as the key to the chamber of divine wealth, the vault that lies beneath your throne. It is not just treasure, Your Majesty. It is the legacy of creation."

The fire crackled louder, as if echoing the intensity of the moment.

The king turned away briefly, gazing toward the distant battlefield where Avyaktakala, the demon of Patal, waited. His thoughts swirled like the rising smoke. He turned-back, voice steady but laced with tension. "And what if I fail? What if I fall to the demon?"

A silence fell over the hill.

The elder scholar stepped forward once more. "If you fall, the sword's power will not perish. It will lie dormant waiting."

"Waiting for what?" Vikrantha asked.

"For the next soul born under your exact astrological conditions," the scholar said. "One born a thousand years from now. Only such a one may claim its full might again."

The king closed his eyes for a long moment. A thousand years. A hope cast far into the unknown. When he opened them again, there was no fear left. Only resolve.

"Then I am the only hope my people have," he said, his voice low but unshakable. "I will not let this world fall. Begin the preparations. We have a war to win."

The scholars bowed, turning to the sacred flame as the chants deepened. In the flickering firelight, King Vikrantha Shura stood motionless, a man about to bear the weight of legend.

CHAPTER EIGHT

THE SWORD OF BLUE FIRE

The sacred flames had died down, but their purpose had only just been fulfilled. In their place now stood a weapon unlike any forged in mortal memory—a blade born not merely of metal and fire, but of spirit and prophecy. It was called **Vyomdhara**, the Sky-Bearer.

The blade itself was translucent, forged from the essence of dragon scale and divine ore, and within its core danced a sliver of fire Vyomdraka's breath, immortalized. It shimmered with a blue aura, not glowing, but pulsing, alive. The hilt was wrapped in celestial thread that shimmered like woven lightning, and above the cross-guard floated a tiny suspended gem, levitating by unseen magic. It whispered to those who looked too long of secrets, of destiny, and of doom.

Vyomdhara was no ordinary weapon. With but a thought, King Vikrantha Shura could vanish, the blade cloaking him in invisibility, rendering him undetectable even to the most cursed demonic senses. Its edge could cleave stone and shatter bone, and its speed rivalled the blink of an eye. To Vikrantha, it felt less like a weapon and more like a part of his own being an extension of his soul, sharpened by fate.

News of the sword's creation spread like wildfire, riding the winds of magic and whispers. And the underworld heard.

Above the peaceful hills of the kingdom, the sky darkened unnaturally. Clouds, black and bloated, coiled like serpents, veiling the sun in a blanket of dread. Thunder cracked like a god's fury. From the far horizon, a terrible line approached dark figures marching in precise silence, cloaked in ash and hatred.

The demon army of **Avyaktakala** had arrived.

They moved like shadows fluid, many-limbed, and clad in corrupted armour that bled smoke. Their weapons dripped with poison that sizzled upon contact with the earth, and their presence alone withered nearby trees and turned grass to ash. They bore no flags, only chaos.

At the heart of this abyssal legion towered Avyaktakala himself—a monstrous titan with armour of obsidian that pulsed with infernal veins. Horns arched like twisted branches from his brow, and his eyes were molten coals of hate. Two wings, skeletal and tattered like ancient scrolls, unfurled behind him, casting massive shadows across the land. Every step he took cracked the ground beneath him.

The battlefield had been chosen: a desolate expanse of scarred earth between the kingdom's last standing watchtower and the jagged ridges of the Demon's Maw. Once a lush valley, now a lifeless plain.

On one side stood the warriors of Vikrantha Shura human, beast, and mage alike armoured in sacred steel and ancient runes. War elephants draped in crimson cloth trumpeted in fury. Archers lined the hills, their bows etched with protection sigils. Spears gleamed under the churning sky, and the thunder of hooves echoed like a heart ready to burst.

On the other side, the demon horde slithered and snarled, an ocean of blasphemous forms. Some crawled with spider-limbs, others towered like living statues of bone. Each step they took poisoned the soil, and a sulfuric mist rolled with them, thick and noxious.

Avyaktakala raised one hand, and his army froze. He spoke no words, his power issued in silence, in domination. His wings flared, casting darkness over the central ridge.

Back on the sacred hill, the monks who had forged Vyomdhara stood in prayer. Their chants, woven into the wind, formed barriers and blessings. Blue light pulsed from their palms and spread across the battlefield, a final gift to the king they had prepared.

Vikrantha Shura rode forth on his white warhorse, now clad in enchanted armour that shimmered under the weight of prophecy. His silver cloak snapped behind him like lightning. Vyomdhara hung at his side, its presence alone making nearby soldiers stand taller, feel braver. Behind him rode his generals, warriors of legend in their own right each knowing this day would be etched into history, or carved into a tomb.

The king paused at the front line. His eyes searched the horizon.

He saw the enemy. He saw the terror. But deeper still, he saw the thread of fate that tied him to this moment. It wasn't just about winning. It was about standing between annihilation and salvation.

The field grew quiet. Wind hissed. Time seemed to still.

And then, rain.

Cold and heavy, it fell from the dark heavens, hissing against armour, soaking flesh and steel alike. The thunder rolled above them like war drums from the gods. Lightning cracked, illuminating both armies in flashes of stark truth.

Vikrantha Shura gripped Vyomdhara's hilt. It hummed beneath his fingers, alive with anticipation.

The war was about to begin.

CHAPTER NINE

The Wrath of Heaven and Hell

As the heavens wept and thunder cracked above, the battle to decide the fate of the kingdom began.

King Vikrantha Shura gave a sharp cry, and the war horns blew through the valley like the roar of ancient beasts. From the hilltops, archers released their arrows in synchronized waves, the skies turning dark with their flight. The frontlines surged soldiers clashing with demons in a frenzy of steel and fire.

The demon horde responded with savage brutality. Blades forged in the abyss slashed through shields, and monstrous limbs crushed men like twigs. The very earth trembled under the weight of the battle, soaked in rain and blood.

Vikrantha Shura plunged into the chaos, Vyomdhara gleaming in his hand like a shard of the sky itself. With every swing, the sword cleaved through demonic flesh and shattered corrupted weapons. It moved like a living thing blazing with blue light, leaving trails of fire through the air. Yet the king felt resistance, not just from the enemy but from within. The sword was powerful, yes but it demanded resolve, demanded purity.

Avyaktakala watched from afar, his burning eyes scanning the battlefield. Then, with a slow, deliberate stretch of his wings, he descended.

He landed like a meteor, the force of his arrival sending shockwaves across the ground. Soldiers and demons alike were thrown aside. Vikrantha turned just in time to see the demon lord raise his obsidian blade, jagged and cruel, and descend upon him.

Their swords met with an explosion of force.

The air cracked. Lightning streaked through the clouds above. Time seemed to slow.

Vikrantha staggered back, feeling the tremble in his arms. Avyaktakala was strong inhumanly so. Again, they clashed, sparks flying as steel met infernal metal. The king used every ounce of strength and skill, but the demon lord seemed unshakable. Blow after blow rained upon him, and Vyomdhara began to flicker with unstable energy.

Blood dripped from the king's brow. He dropped to one knee, gasping. The enemy's laughter rumbled like thunder.

"Is this your champion?" Avyaktakala roared. "Your last hope? He bleeds like all the rest."

The words echoed, pressing down like a curse. But within that moment of pain, Vikrantha remembered the monks' voices. The chants. The fire. The dragon's sacrifice. The legacy.

He closed his eyes.

And vanished.

The battlefield gasped.

Using Vyomdhara's power of invisibility, Vikrantha moved like a ghost. Avyaktakala swung wildly, trying to anticipate the king's strike, but the sword had bonded with its master. In silence, Vikrantha reappeared behind the demon and drove Vyomdhara into his side.

A howl split the sky.

Avyaktakala turned with inhuman speed, catching the king by the throat and lifting him from the ground. Black fire burned across his wounded side, but his rage had only grown. "You think your tricks can stop destiny?" he spat.

Vikrantha struggled, vision dimming.

Then he remembered the blade's promise: It wasn't just a weapon. It was *his will.*

With a roar of defiance, he forced Vyomdhara upward, its blue light exploding across the field. In one final motion, he became invisible once more, slipped from the demon's grip, and emerged behind him—driving the sword deep into Avyaktakala's neck.

The demon's scream shattered the sky.

A blast of energy erupted from the wound, throwing Vikrantha backward. The demon staggered, clutching at his throat, as black flames consumed his body. He fell to his knees.

And with a final growl of hate—collapsed.

Silence followed. Then cheers. so many voices rising in unison that the heavens themselves seemed to echo back.

The battle was over.

CHAPTER TEN

THE AWAKENING OF DESTINY

The storm of ancient war had faded into memory, and the story of King Vikrantha Shura had drawn to its legendary end. As Arav stood there, breathless and wide-eyed, the monk beside him remained composed, the weight of time etched into the lines of his face.

Arav, his voice still trembling from the vision he had just witnessed, turned to the monk and asked, "If the king defeated the demon... if he won... why do you need me now? Isn't everything over?"

The monk looked at him with calm gravity. His eyes, ancient and deep like forgotten oceans, held something that words could not fully explain.

"Yes," he said slowly, "it was over—**then**. But evil never truly dies. It sleeps. It waits. And now... the descendants of the demon Avyaktakala have returned. They rise not from the ashes of war, but from the shadows of time. The seal of peace weakens. You, Arav, were born under the same celestial signs as the king. You carry the same fate. And now, you must awaken to it."

The words settled heavily in Arav's chest. A thousand questions bloomed in his mind, but only one escaped his lips.

"Where is the sword now?" he asked.

The monk's lips curled into a faint smile. "Come. It is time you saw it for yourself."

They journeyed under the cloak of night, moving through dense woods and past ancient stone paths that seemed untouched by modern hands. The stars above glittered strangely, as though aware of the path Arav now walked. The deeper they went, the more the world around him seemed to blur into something surreal less like a hike through the hills and more like stepping into a memory carved into the land itself.

Finally, they reached it.

An enormous stone gate stood nestled between two cliffs, veiled in moss and vines. Symbols older than language were etched into its face, and a subtle humming filled the air, as if the stones breathed in rhythm with the Earth.

Around the entrance, cloaked figures stood still as statues monks, each clad in robes of deep indigo, silent guardians of a time-forgotten secret. Arav's skin tingled as he looked at them. Their eyes gleamed, but they said nothing.

The monk who had brought him stepped forward and placed his palm on a flat panel carved into the gate.

He whispered a chant, his voice soft but resonant:

"Vyomam dware... chhidrayati shakti... prabodha!"

At his words, the carvings began to glow with soft blue light. The gate trembled, then split apart with a deep, echoing rumble. Inside lay a corridor lit by floating torches, their flames an ethereal blue.

"Come," the monk said again.

They stepped inside, descending a spiral staircase that felt carved by gods. The air grew heavier, denser with every step. When they reached the bottom, Arav's breath caught in his throat.

Before him lay an enormous subterranean chamber, its walls covered in murals that shimmered with starlight. Painted stories of dragons, of kings, of wars and victories wrapped the dome-like cavern in a living chronicle of a world long gone.

At the center of the chamber stood a stone dais, upon which rested a sword unlike anything Arav had ever imagined.

Vyomdhara.

The sword gleamed even in the absence of light, bathed in an eternal blue aura. The blade was translucent, almost glass-like, yet it pulsed with impossible strength. Within its core swirled a flame the immortal breath of the dragon Vyomdraka. The hilt, wrapped in celestial thread, shimmered like sunlight on water, and above the cross-guard floated the same tiny gem Arav had seen in the vision. It levitated without support, spinning gently.

Arav took a step forward. As he approached, he felt a sudden change.

The air thickened. The room dimmed.

And then, the world shifted.

Before he could utter a word, the cave transformed. The murals on the walls began to move, as if time itself had peeled open. The still monks surrounding the chamber transformed into armoured warriors. The glowing torches flared brighter. The scent of fire and steel filled the air. Horses neighed in the distance. War horns echoed like thunder.

Arav's eyes widened.

He was no longer in the cave, he was standing in the past.

He spun around in awe. All around him was a war camp from another age. Tents billowed in the wind. Soldiers trained with swords that sparked with energy. And above it all, the castle of King Vikrantha Shura loomed in the distance, its spires touching the sky.

But then, the illusion faded. Like a wave, the vision withdrew, and the stillness returned. The monks were monks again. The cave was quiet. The murals were still.

Arav stumbled back, breathless. "What... what just happened?"

The monk placed a hand on his shoulder. "The sword shows you what was, and what might be again. It recognizes you. It tests you. You have seen a glimpse of the world you now belong to."

Arav looked at Vyomdhara once more. This time, the sword did not just shine. It called.

"This," said the monk, "is not merely a weapon. It is a responsibility. One that was forged for a king, and now waits for its next bearer."

Arav could not look away. He felt it deep within the fire of destiny beginning to burn.

THE FIRST SPARK OF WAR

The cool night breeze rustled the curtains as Arav lay on his bed, his eyes open, staring into the ceiling as if it held all the questions in the world. The events of the day replayed endlessly in his mind. the monk's transformation, the incredible tale of King Vikrantha Shura, the sword forged from a dragon's breath, and the cave sealed away with sacred chants.

His fingers still trembled from the touch of the sword. Even in memory, Vyomdhara's blue aura radiated like a second sun. And the moment the ancient chamber opened, revealing monks guarding the sword like sacred flame, he couldn't shake the surrealness of it all. The air had smelled of incense and power, time itself seeming to hang thick in the stone-walled sanctum. It felt less like walking into a cave and more like stepping back a thousand years.

And yet here he was back in his ordinary bedroom, with his textbooks scattered on the study table and his alarm clock ticking toward dawn.

"Why me?" he whispered, rolling onto his side.

Before long, the weight of fatigue overtook his restless mind, and he drifted into sleep, still half-dreaming of winged demons and warriors of fire.

The next morning, his alarm blared like a trumpet of war. Arav groaned, slapped it silent, and sat up. A part of him expected to find himself still in the cave, standing before Vyomdhara. But everything looked normal. Too normal. As if none of it had happened.

But that illusion shattered the moment he arrived at college.

The morning sun filtered through the college gates, casting a warm glow over the crowd of students entering with backpacks and chai cups. Arav greeted a few friends half-heartedly, still fogged by yesterday's memories.

That's when he saw them.

A group of figures tall, strangely dressed, faces obscured beneath cowls of dark grey moved unnaturally through the campus. Their presence sent an instant chill through Arav's spine. No one else seemed to notice them. But Arav knew. These were not humans. Their forms shimmered with a subtle distortion, like heatwaves bending the air.

One of them turned. Eyes like glowing embers locked onto Arav.

He turned and ran.

His heartbeat thundered in his ears as he pushed past students, dashing through corridors and leaping down staircases. The world blurred. Behind him, the creatures hissed and followed, inhumanly fast.

A hand seized his shoulder, pulling him into the shadows. Arav spun, ready to fight until he saw the monk.

Parivrajaka's eyes were serious but calm. "The time has come. But you are not ready for war."

"I... I didn't know they'd come this soon!" Arav gasped, still catching his breath.

The monk led him to an alley where the creatures couldn't follow. "The descendants of Avyaktakala have sensed your awakening. They will not wait. But you... you're soft. Weak. Just a boy who's been told stories."

Arav felt the sting of those words, but he stood tall. "Then make me strong. Train me."

Parivrajaka narrowed his eyes, searching Arav's resolve. "Training will break your body. Tear your muscles. Burn your spirit. And even then, it might not be enough."

"I'll do it. But only after college hours. My parents can't know. Not yet."

The monk paused, then nodded. "So be it. Come to the hill after sunset. We begin today."

The training grounds were unlike anything Arav had imagined. Hidden behind a forest veil near the old ruins above the city, the area seemed shielded from the modern world. Ancient statues lined the rocky paths, their eyes weathered but watchful. In the center was a circle of earth surrounded by tall, aged trees like an arena untouched by time.

Parivrajaka waited, clad in simple robes, a wooden staff in hand. Around him were training dummies, weapons of all kinds, and stones stacked in impossible patterns.

"Strength isn't just in arms and legs," the monk began. "It begins in the mind. In pain. In will."

The first week was a torment.

Arav returned every evening, dropping his bag at the foot of the hill before stepping into the ancient world. Parivrajaka pushed him to the edge running up hills with heavy stones strapped to his back, lifting logs until his shoulders screamed, standing on one leg for hours to train his balance. Every fall was followed by a demand to rise. Every wince met with, "Again."

He learned to fight with bare hands first stances, blocks, the art of using his opponent's force. Then came the weapons. Staffs. Spears. Blades carved from stone. Each day a new discipline. Each night he returned home, battered but more determined.

There were moments he wanted to quit when his knees gave out, when the bruises became too much, when the sword in his dreams seemed more like a curse than a destiny. But Parivrajaka would simply say, "Vikrantha Shura bled too. And he never stopped."

In time, Arav began to change. His body grew leaner, his posture more-firm. He could now climb the boulder slope without pause, disarm a dummy in seconds, and catch arrows mid-flight. His senses sharpened. His dreams grew clearer.

One night, as he lay exhausted beneath the stars, Parivrajaka sat beside him.

"You're beginning to remember, aren't you?"

Arav nodded slowly. "Flashes. I see the battlefield. The blue sword. Fire. Wings."

The monk's voice softened. "Your soul remembers what the world has forgotten. That is why you must rise not just as a warrior, but as a guardian."

Arav looked up at the sky, where the moon gleamed like the eye of destiny.

The war hadn't begun yet. But his training had. And so had the countdown.

CHAPTER TWELVE

THE FIRST KILL

Training had become a ritual, a part of Arav's life as natural as breathing. By day, he was just another college student blending into the crowd. By night, he was something else entirely a warrior in the making, hardened by sweat, pain, and the teachings of an immortal monk.

But no amount of training could have prepared him for what came next.

It was a quiet night, the kind that usually brought Arav some peace after a day of intense routines. He stood at the balcony of his room, staring at the stars. The wind carried with it a strange scent faintly metallic, almost like burning coal. He frowned and scanned the street below.

Nothing.

Then he felt it.

A cold chill danced down his spine. The kind of instinctual alarm that no logic could ignore. He turned slowly, hesitantly and there it was. A figure stood just behind him inside the room, tall and crooked, its skin a pale shade of grayish green, eyes like molten lava. A low, guttural growl vibrated through the air.

A demon.

Arav's instincts kicked in. He dove forward, rolled, and grabbed the stick he'd started keeping beside his bed. Without hesitation, he burst out of the room and sprinted down the staircase, not even stopping to shut the door behind him. He couldn't risk his family getting hurt.

The demon followed, silent as smoke, slipping down the walls and gliding through the shadows. Arav ran through the empty streets, heart pounding, legs burning. He needed to get away somewhere isolated, somewhere he could fight without risking innocent lives.

The old construction site on the city outskirts.

It took everything he had to reach it. The site was deserted, a skeletal framework of steel rods and broken concrete. Arav darted between rusting pillars, finally turning to face his pursuer.

The demon crept forward, claws gleaming in the moonlight. It hissed something in an ancient tongue—a promise of death.

But Arav wasn't the same boy who once trembled in fear.

He remembered the monk's words, the discipline etched into his muscles over weeks of relentless training. He steadied his breath, raised his guard, and charged.

The fight was brutal. Arav ducked under a sweeping claw, landed a punch to the demon's ribs, and rolled away before the creature's tail could impale him. It was fast far faster than anything he'd sparred with. And strong.

He took hit after hit, his limbs screaming from the impact. Blood trickled from his temple, and he could feel a rib crack. For a moment, he faltered. The demon struck, slamming him into a wall. Arav gasped, struggling to rise.

"You're not ready," it growled, stepping closer.

But that's when it happened.

In that instant of desperation, something inside Arav ignited. The blue glow returned. His skin shimmered faintly, and he could feel energy rushing through his veins like wildfire. The memory of the sword, the legacy of Vikrantha Shura, it surged within him.

The demon lunged.

But Arav vanished.

He reappeared behind it, instinctively activating the ability to turn invisible. The demon spun, confused, just in time for Arav to grab a rusted steel rod and drive it through the beast's back with a roar.

The demon shrieked, its body convulsing before turning into ash, vanishing into the wind as if it had never been there.

Arav stood still, panting, bleeding, stunned.

He had done it.

He had killed one of the underlings of the demon's descendants.

The realization washed over him slowly. He wasn't just a boy training for a war, he was now part of it. The threat was real. The enemies were here. And his victory tonight meant more than just survival.

He walked back home as dawn began to break, his shirt torn, his body aching.

But inside, a fire had been lit.

He could win.

He *would* win.

CHAPTER THIRTEEN

SHADOWS IN THE DAYLIGHT

The days grew darker, not because of the sun or weather, but because of the weight Arav now carried. Each sunrise came with a new battle hidden within ordinary moments, he was a student by name, but a warrior by necessity. The demon army, descendants of the ancient darkness that once threatened the earth, had begun to hunt him. Not just at night. Not in the shadows alone. But in the daylight, in places teeming with people.

It began subtly.

At college, he noticed a janitor who never seemed to clean. The man would stand for hours near the library's edge, unmoving, eyes glazed over as if watching from another world. Then, at the park, a woman in tattered clothing sat for hours, never blinking. Their eyes glowed faintly-red, unnatural. Arav had begun to recognize the signs. These were not humans. These were demons, cloaked in illusion.

They followed him. Every time he left a class, turned a corner, or sat at the edge of the campus lawns to sip tea with his friends, he could feel their gaze. It was only a matter of time before they attacked.

And they did.

In the quiet corners of empty stairwells, in deserted parking lots, and in the abandoned metro station late at night. They came at him in ones and twos, never revealing themselves in public. Arav fought them all some with raw skill, others with instinct, and often with sheer willpower. Each encounter left him bruised, bloodied, but victorious.

His training had become more secretive and disciplined than ever. At midnight, long after his family was asleep, he would sneak out of his home. The city's silence was his ally. He'd walk past closed shops and silent buildings, reach the edge of the old woods, and meet the monk Parivrajaka waiting under the same banyan tree.

There, the real transformation took place.

"You must learn not just to fight, but to endure," the monk would say. And so, he did. Arav was trained in martial arts, taught how to read movement, react to instinct, and hone his reflexes. His body was pushed beyond limits, running barefoot through bramble paths, sparring until his muscles failed, and holding stances under freezing waterfalls to discipline his mind.

Pain was his constant companion. But so was growth.

"They're testing you," the monk warned one night, as they stood atop a cliff, the moon casting silvery light on the forest below. "The true descendant of Avyaktakala has not arrived yet. These are scouts, soldiers. They seek your weakness."

Arav looked at his bloodied fists. "And if I fail?"

"Then the sword remains buried. And your world falls."

He nodded, the weight settling on him like armour. There was no room for fear anymore.

As weeks passed, the attacks became more frequent. In the chemistry lab, a student beside him suddenly erupted into demonic form, eyes glowing, hands transforming into claws. Arav barely managed to push him out of the emergency exit before anyone else could see. At the park, a street performer turned mid-juggle and launched himself at Arav. They tumbled into the fountain, water splashing, and Arav emerged with another victory hidden behind soaked clothes and trembling breath.

But the toll grew heavier.

He barely slept. His marks at college dropped. Friends began to worry about the dark circles under his eyes, his jumpy reactions. But he couldn't afford explanations. How could he tell them he was the chosen protector of a thousand-year legacy?

Still, he endured. Because every night, as he gripped the training weapons under the monk's guidance, every cut and bruise reminded him of his purpose. He wasn't just fighting for himself anymore. He was guarding his world.

One evening, after a particularly violent battle behind the college canteen where he had shattered a demon's skull with a rusted pipe, he sat on the rooftop alone. The city lights blinked like stars on the ground. He watched them, exhausted.

"Why do they keep coming?" he asked the air, voice hoarse.

The monk appeared beside him, as if summoned by his despair. "Because they fear you. They know what you are becoming."

"And what is that?"

"A warrior destined to end their bloodline."

Arav looked at his hands, the dried blood caked along his knuckles. "Sometimes, I think I'm losing myself."

"No," the monk said softly. "You are finding the part of you that was hidden. Buried under books and laughter. This is your truth."

Arav didn't respond. But deep down, he knew. He had changed.

In the shadows, he was no longer the hunted.

He was becoming the hunter.

THE RISING STORM

The sky over the city turned an unnatural shade of grey. Clouds coiled like serpents, thunder crackled without rain, and a tense pressure filled the air as if the world itself was holding its breath. Far from human eyes, deep in the underworld realm where shadows whispered and evil brooded, the true descendant of Avyaktakala had been watching. His crimson eyes scanned the veil between dimensions, observing the string of failed attempts to stop Arav.

Each of his demon soldiers had fallen. One by one. Despite their stealth, their power, and their cunning, the boy had survived. Not just survived, he had grown stronger. The descendant, cloaked in midnight-black armour laced with pulsing red veins of dark magic, rose from his throne of bones and snarled.

"Enough. No more delays. He must be destroyed now."

With a wave of his clawed hand, portals ignited across the human realm. And war began.

It was the end of a long day at college. Students poured out of lecture halls, laughing, stretching, checking their phones, and complaining about assignments. Arav was among them, exhausted but relieved to be done. His muscles ached from the midnight training, his mind still replaying the last battle he had fought just two nights ago. He stepped through the college gates, his backpack slung casually over his shoulder, when the ground beneath him trembled.

At first, he thought it was a minor quake. But then came a loud rumble like a thousand drums beating together. Students screamed as the earth cracked. Pavement split open, and dark smoke erupted from beneath. Buildings shuddered; glass shattered. From the torn earth emerged towering figures, armoured in darkness, their eyes glowing like dying stars.

People panicked. Chaos took over. Cars crashed, crowds stampeded in all directions, teachers yelled in vain, and the city became a whirlpool of terror.

Arav's eyes widened as he saw them an entire legion of demons marching through the city center. And at their lead, rising like a dark god, was the true descendant of Avyaktakala.

He stood nearly ten feet tall, muscles like granite, his cape made from shadows themselves. Two massive horns spiralled from his head, and his voice, when it spoke, echoed across the skyline.

"So... you're the chosen one? The boy with a sword and a bedtime curfew?" he sneered, smirking down at Arav. "Impressive. You've survived longer than I expected."

Arav stood frozen. For a second, fear gripped him, this wasn't like the other demons. This was different. Ancient. Angry. Powerful beyond compare.

But before Arav could react, a bright flash appeared beside him. Parivrajaka the monk landed like lightning, his robes swirling in the wind.

"Arav! This is it. The final war has begun."

"Now?! In the middle of the city?!"

The monk nodded. "They want panic. Destruction. This is how they win through fear."

Suddenly, the demon king raised his arm and launched a wave of dark energy. It struck near Arav, throwing him backward into the campus wall. Dust flew. Students screamed. Arav coughed, dazed.

The demon laughed. "You're not ready. You never were."

Before Arav could rise, the demon stomped toward him and with a swift motion, struck him across the chest. The blow sent Arav flying through the college gates, landing hard on the street.

His friends Anjali, Rishi, and Prateek stood just nearby, watching in horror.

"Arav!" they screamed, running toward him.

"Stay back!" he called, struggling to his feet. His body ached, ribs burning, vision blurred. But he stood. The demon advanced, conjuring a sword of fire.

Arav clenched his fists. He looked around. The city was crumbling. The air was thick with cries and smoke. And he... he was the only hope.

With a roar, he summoned Vyomdhara—the invisible sword.

The blade materialized into his hand, glowing blue with a fiery core. Instantly, he vanished from sight. The demon paused, momentarily confused. Then a slash a blur of blue light ripped across the demon's shoulder. Blood hissed into steam.

Arav reappeared behind him, breathing heavily.

"I'm not the same boy from yesterday."

The battle ignited.

Steel met claw. Fire clashed with blue light. The demon's power was monstrous every strike from him tore the earth, shattered stone, and sent shockwaves across the battlefield. But Arav dodged with increasing precision, using his training, his pain, and his rage.

His friends watched from behind rubble, stunned, mouths agape. The boy they knew the shy, funny, quiet Arav was now dancing between death and destiny.

The demon grabbed a car and hurled it. Arav leapt, sliced it in half mid-air, and landed with a roll. The blade hummed, sensing his will. He turned invisible again, appearing near the demon's side and striking deep into his leg. The demon roared, stumbling.

"You dare?!" the creature growled. "You are still just a boy!"

Arav didn't answer. He channelled everything his fear, anger, and purpose into his next strike. He vanished, reappeared behind the demon, and sliced clean through the creature's back. Dark blood spilled.

But the demon was far from finished. He slammed Arav with a shadow-fist that sent him crashing into a bus. Pain screamed through his bones.

"Enough!" the demon howled. "I'll end you now!"

He raised his weapon, preparing the final strike. Arav lay motionless.

Then he heard voices. His friends. Their fear. Their cries.

He opened his eyes. Through the pain, through the dust and blood, he saw them watching. And he remembered who he was.

He stood.

With every ounce of strength left, he surged forward, becoming a blur of light. Vyomdhara glowed brighter than ever. The demon swung but Arav ducked, spun, leapt onto his back, and with one last war cry, drove the blade through the demon's neck.

Time seemed to freeze.

The sky cracked. A flash of light. Then silence.

The demon's eyes widened in disbelief. He fell to his knees, gurgled a final curse, and dissolved into black mist.

The war was over.

For now.

CHAPTER FIFTEEN

SILENCE AFTER THE STORM

Smoke curled into the sky like dark prayers, rising from the battlefield that had once been Arav's college courtyard. Now, it was unrecognizable charred, scorched, and smeared with the echoes of war. The scent of ash and iron hung heavy in the air, mixing with the metallic sting of blood. It was over.

Arav stood at the center of the ruins, his chest rising and falling with laboured breaths. His shirt was torn, soaked in sweat and blood some his own, some not. Vyomdhara, the invisible sword that had once gleamed like a beacon, now rested quietly in his hand, pulsing with faint blue light. The weapon that had once belonged to King Vikrantha Shura, forged from dragon flame and celestial will, had served its purpose once again.

The ground beneath his feet was littered with broken weapons, scorched earth, and bodies. His comrades those warriors who had trained silently in the shadows, those who stood beside him in the last stand lay lifeless around him. Their sacrifice, noble and complete.

Only the monk remained.

Parivrajaka walked through the silent battlefield, his robes still untouched by dirt or blood, as though the chaos of war respected his sanctity. He stopped beside Arav, placing a gentle hand on his shoulder. "You did it," the monk whispered, eyes glinting with both sorrow and pride.

Arav exhaled deeply, a breath that felt like it had been held since the war began. His legs shook beneath him, and he dropped to his knees. The silence screamed louder than the clash of swords had.

"They're all gone," Arav murmured, looking at the fallen warriors, some still with their weapons clutched in their stiff hands. "They gave everything."

The monk nodded solemnly. "Yes. And because of them, the world breathes free again."

It began slowly. People who had been hiding in nearby buildings started to emerge students, professors, civilians. They stepped cautiously onto the war-torn grounds, their faces pale with awe and confusion. Their eyes landed on Arav, the lone survivor standing amid the ruins, holding a sword that shimmered with ethereal light.

Whispers filled the air.

"That's him..."

"He saved us..."

"Arav... he fought them all... he won."

Cameras were pulled from pockets. Phones began to record. In minutes, the story began to spread across social media and news channels of a boy who turned into a warrior, of a battle no one could explain, and of a victory that saved hundreds of lives.

Reporters arrived, confused and breathless, pushing microphones toward him. Drones hovered above, capturing the scene from every angle. But Arav barely heard them. His mind was still with the fallen.

He stood slowly, the sword still at his side. He didn't offer statements. He didn't answer questions. He simply turned to the monk, who gave him a nod of understanding.

They walked away from the battlefield together.

Later that evening, Arav sat on the rooftop of his home. The air was still, eerily calm. Below, the world was still buzzing with the aftermath of what had happened. His phone was filled with messages, missed calls, news headlines, and friend requests. He had become a legend overnight.

But fame meant nothing to him.

He looked at the sword, now resting beside him. In the starlight, Vyomdhara shimmered faintly, its aura still alive but subdued as if it, too, was grieving.

The monk appeared behind him, silent as always.

"Why me?" Arav asked after a long pause. "Why was I the one who had to survive?"

Parivrajaka sat beside him. "Because destiny chooses not by ease, but by strength. Your heart was ready, even when your body wasn't. Now the world knows."

"They look at me like I'm a hero. But I couldn't save them all."

"No hero saves everyone. A true hero fights knowing that he might lose everything and still chooses to fight."

Arav was quiet for a long time. Below, fire trucks were still dousing smoking remnants, and medics tended to survivors. But here, above the chaos, the sky was finally clear.

"What happens now?" he asked.

The monk stood, brushing dust from his robes. "Now, you live. You carry their memory forward. And when the time comes again and it will you will be ready."

Arav watched him walk away, his figure slowly disappearing into the night. The silence lingered, comforting and cold.

He turned to look at the sword again.

CHAPTER SIXTEEN

A NEW DAWN

The days after the great war passed slowly, like ripples in a lake after a boulder had fallen. Silence filled the air. The kind of silence that was not just the absence of sound, but the echo of lives lost, of dreams buried beneath ashes and battlefields. Arav had won the war. He had slain the descendant, ended the demonic bloodline, and ensured the survival of humanity. But as the smoke cleared and the bodies vanished into memory, only he and the monk remained.

They stood amidst the ruins. The warriors who had stood with him were gone some fallen in battle, others returned to the spirit realm from which they were summoned. The once furious battleground was now a wasteland of scorched soil and broken weapons. Yet, it was over. The curse had lifted.

For days, Arav stayed home, locked away in silence. He didn't feel like returning to college, didn't want to face the normal world. What was the point of lectures, jokes, and meaningless chatter after facing death, after watching friends and foes fall before his eyes? The walls of his room were the only place he felt safe, the only place where he could quietly mourn and reflect.

His parents, though unaware of the truth behind his wounds and his silence, saw his pain. They thought it was grief from some unknown trauma, a loss perhaps. They didn't pry. Instead, they gently encouraged him.

"You've always been strong, Arav," his mother said one morning. "But life must go on. Maybe going back to college will help distract you. Help you heal."

His father added, "It's not about forgetting, son. It's about living. You must not let whatever is haunting you win."

After some resistance, Arav finally gave in. The next day, he put on his college uniform, brushed his hair back, and left his house. But as he walked through the gates, everything felt strange.

The same corridors, the same trees, the same scent of old cement and fresh-cut grass but something was different. People were staring. Not with ridicule, not with judgement. But with admiration. With reverence.

A group of students greeted him with nods and smiles. Someone whispered, "That's Arav... the one who saved everyone."

Even his old tormentors those who once laughed at him, excluded him, mocked him now approached him with softened eyes.

"Hey Arav," one said, scratching the back of his neck awkwardly, "we were wrong about you. Sorry for being jerks."

Another chimed in, "You're... something else, man. What you did, even if we don't fully get it, we know it was real."

Teachers smiled. Classmates whispered. No one pushed him, no one joked. They all looked at him like he was something beyond human. And maybe, in a way, he was.

But to Arav, it all felt distant like he was watching it through a foggy glass. The world that had once ignored him had now turned around. Yet it no longer mattered. Their words, their praises, they couldn't reach the place inside him that still ached. A place hollowed out by loss, by responsibility, by power.

After a few hours, he left the campus early, walking alone through the quieter streets of the city. He didn't know where he was headed only that he needed to move, to breathe.

As he wandered into a quieter part of town, something caught his eye. A group of rowdy young men were crowding around a woman at the edge of the road. She looked terrified, clutching her bag, trying to step back, but they blocked her path.

Arav didn't think. His body moved before his mind could.

He dashed across the road.

"Hey!" he shouted, his voice sharp and commanding.

The men turned, laughing, sneering.

"What are you gonna do, hero boy? This isn't your movie."

But they didn't know who they were dealing with.

In seconds, Arav was upon them. His reflexes honed by months of brutal training kicked in. He struck the first man with the heel of his palm, sending him crashing to the pavement. The second lunged at him, but Arav sidestepped and used the man's momentum to flip him over his shoulder.

The rest tried to flee, but Arav caught one more by the collar and growled, "Remember her face. If she ever sees you again, you'll see me."

The remaining two scattered.

Arav turned to the woman, offering his hand. "Are you okay?"

She nodded, stunned, tears in her eyes. "Thank you. Thank you so much."

Arav nodded gently and walked away without waiting for praise. Something had clicked inside him during that moment something powerful.

He realized then: his purpose didn't end with the war. It began there.

There would always be evil in the world. Maybe not in the form of demons with fangs and fire but cruelty, injustice, fear. It wore many masks. But he had the strength now to fight it.

That night, as he sat on his rooftop under the stars, he looked out at the city lights so much like the battlefield after the smoke cleared.

He whispered to the wind, "I may have ended a war, but this world... this world needs more than a sword. It needs a protector."

And Arav knew, deep down, that he had found something stronger than power.

He had found purpose.

CHAPTER SEVENTEEN

The Strength of Purpose

Days turned into weeks after the war. Arav had seen the battlefield, had fought with demons, and had emerged not only as a warrior but as a symbol of courage and resilience. The scars on his body had begun to heal, but the ones etched into his soul still throbbed in silence. He was no longer the boy who once worried about college assignments and social awkwardness. He was something more something awakened.

His parents noticed the change in him. There was a calm, a maturity in his eyes that hadn't been there before. Though he smiled at them, it rarely reached his eyes. They supported him, gently encouraging him to return to normal life. After all, the war was over. Peace had returned.

Eventually, Arav agreed. He began to go out again, walking through the city that he had once saved from a fate none even knew had existed. And it was on those walks that he began to see the world differently.

It began one evening in a narrow alley behind a busy market. He heard a scream a desperate cry for help. Arav rushed in and found a young boy, no older than ten, trapped beneath a fallen vegetable cart. The vendor had collapsed in panic, unable to lift it. Without a word, Arav stepped in. With strength honed through endless battles and training, he lifted the cart like it was made of feathers and pulled the child to safety.

People surrounded him, clapping, thanking, praising. Arav simply nodded and walked away. He hadn't done it for applause. He had done it because it was needed.

The next incident came just two days later.

A car had spun out of control and crashed into a pole on a busy street. Flames licked the edges of the engine, and the driver was trapped inside, unconscious. A crowd had formed, everyone too afraid to act. Arav didn't hesitate. He rushed forward, broke the glass window with a swift elbow, unbuckled the man, and carried him to safety just seconds before the engine exploded into a ball of fire.

He stayed with the man until the ambulance arrived, then disappeared into the crowd before anyone could ask his name.

Word began to spread. Stories of a mysterious young man helping people in miraculous ways strong, fast, fearless began circulating online and in newspapers. Videos surfaced of Arav saving lives, always leaving before he could be thanked.

But Arav didn't do it for fame.

He had found something else.

Purpose.

He realized he could be more than a sword-bearer of ancient prophecy. He could be a protector of the present. Not every battle needed a sword. Some required presence. Some needed strength of heart. And he had both.

One rainy afternoon, he was walking past a narrow bridge when he saw a man standing on the edge, looking down into the river. The man's shoulders were slumped, his body tense. People passed by, but no one noticed. No one saw the pain. But Arav did.

He walked up and stood beside the man in silence. After a few moments, he said, "It's never the end. Not really. The pain... it's just a shadow. But the sun will rise again. Always."

The man looked at him, eyes brimming with tears. "I've lost everything."

Arav nodded. "So, did I. And I thought it was over. But then I found that helping someone else brought me back. Let me help you."

They talked for hours, under the shelter of a tea stall nearby. And when the man left, his eyes held hope. Just a spark. But it was enough.

Soon, Arav made helping others a part of his life. He worked quietly, staying out of the limelight, assisting in orphanages, protecting the bullied, aiding injured animals, and calming those in distress. He used his training, his strength, his speed but most importantly, his compassion.

He was no longer just Arav the warrior.

He was Arav the guardian.

He began working with local shelters, helping reconstruct damaged neighbourhoods silently affected by demonic skirmishes. He used his influence though never publicly to push for better safety measures in public places. He donated anonymously to schools needing books and helped kids train in self-defence during late evenings.

The monk, Parivrajaka, watched all of this with silent pride.

One night, under the same banyan tree where his training had begun, the monk said, "You have become more than I had hoped."

Arav smiled faintly. "I still feel like I'm just beginning."

"That's the sign of a true protector," the monk replied. "The battle may be over, but peace must be protected. Not with swords, but with strength. You've understood that."

Arav looked up at the night sky. "I don't know what the future holds. But I know one thing now I can make a difference. Even if it's just one person at a time."

The monk nodded. "And sometimes, that's enough to change the world."

CHAPTER EIGHTEEN

SHADOWS OF PRIDE

Arav's days of service to the city and its people grew longer and more intense. He moved like a silent guardian, appearing in moments of chaos, resolving conflicts, and vanishing before praise could be offered. Whether it was rescuing an old woman from a house fire or stopping a group of thieves in a dark alley, Arav seemed unstoppable invincible.

At first, his work was driven by purpose. A sense of duty. The memory of the war, of the fallen warriors, still clung to him like a second skin. But slowly, without realizing it, his motives began to shift.

Where once he acted with humility, now a seed of pride began to grow.

It started subtly. After stopping a robbery at a local jewellery store, the store owner tried to reward him with money. Arav declined as usual but this time, he lingered. He enjoyed the way the crowd looked at him. He listened longer to their praises. A part of him began to crave it.

As the days passed, he began to look for trouble not to prevent it, but to prove himself. To show the world that he was beyond ordinary.

He hunted down local criminals, pickpockets, small-time thugs, street-level gangs. But his methods grew harsh. Where he once disarmed and warned, he now delivered bruises. Broken bones. Pain.

"Justice," he told himself. "I'm doing what the system can't."

One night, he encountered a gang breaking into a warehouse. They were unarmed teenagers, just trying to steal electronics. He didn't listen to their pleas. Rage consumed him. He fought like a storm, his fists relentless. When one of the boys cried out in agony, Arav didn't stop. He struck harder.

When it was over, the boys lay broken, crying for mercy. Arav stood above them, breath heavy, knuckles bloodied. There were no cheers that night. No thanks. Just silence. And distant sirens.

He disappeared before the authorities arrived.

The monk, Parivrajaka, watched this transformation with growing concern. He knew power could corrupt, even the noblest heart.

"He is walking a dangerous path," he whispered one evening as he lit a prayer lamp beneath the temple tree. "From protector to judge. From guardian to executioner."

Arav continued. He stopped using words. He didn't listen to explanations. Every thief, every criminal he saw them not as people, but as enemies. Enemies to be punished.

One afternoon, he came across a man stealing from a fruit vendor. Arav didn't ask why. He pulled the man aside, and with a single strike, dislocated his shoulder.

"What have you become?" the vendor whispered in fear, backing away. "You're not saving people anymore... you're punishing them."

Arav said nothing.

He returned home that night and stared at his reflection. His eyes, once bright with purpose, were darker now. His face, sharper. His soul, heavier.

Still, he told himself: "They deserved it. I did what was right."

But the line between right and wrong was beginning to blur.

At college, students kept their distance. Though they greeted him with respect, there was a fear behind their smiles. Arav could sense it. Even his closest friends struggled to connect with him. They no longer saw a hero. They saw someone unpredictable. Dangerous. His nightly training continued, but even the monk noticed the change.

"Arav," Parivrajaka said during one session, "power is a blade. Sharpen it with humility, or it will cut you from within."

Arav didn't respond. He simply swung harder, faster, against the training post, splintering it in two.

He couldn't stop. Not now. The world was full of darkness, and he was the only light.

Or so he believed.

But deep inside, the whispers began.

Whispers of doubt.

Whispers of something darker.

CHAPTER NINETEEN

The Fall of Light

Arav stood atop a rooftop, overlooking the city he'd once sworn to protect. His breathing was slow, measured, but heavy with thoughts that weighed on his chest like anchors. The stars above sparkled like indifferent eyes, distant and cold. For weeks now, he had taken justice into his own hands dispensing it not with reason, but with rage. He convinced himself it was necessary. That he was above systems, above failure.

But the city had begun to whisper.

People no longer spoke his name with admiration. Fear had replaced awe. Respect had withered into caution. Even those he once saved avoided his gaze. Children no longer waved when he passed. Friends no longer approached.

He told himself it didn't matter. That they didn't understand what he carried.

Until the day his own friends turned against him.

It happened when he tried to punish a known gangster who had been terrorizing a local neighbourhood. This time, he didn't hold back, he beat the man until he stopped moving. But when he turned, expecting gratitude, he saw his friends standing there.

They hadn't come to support him. They had come to stop him.

"You're not a saviour anymore, Arav," one of them said. "You've become something else."

The words hit harder than any punch he had thrown. That night, he wandered the city aimlessly, unsure of himself, of his actions, of his very purpose. Everything he fought for, everything he believed in, seemed to shatter into a thousand sharp pieces.

By midnight, there was only one place he could go, the temple.

The monk Parivrajaka sat beneath the Bodhi tree, eyes closed, his breath calm like a still pond. Arav approached him like a wounded animal, pride swallowed, his voice weak.

"Master... I don't know who I am anymore. I need a solution. Tell me what to do."

The monk opened his eyes slowly. There was no anger in them—only sadness.

"You ask for a solution, but there is only one. I must take your powers back. It is the only way to restore balance."

Arav flinched, as though struck. "All of them? But..."

"There is no other way. Your strength has become your prison. Your heart is clouded. Without clarity, you are a danger to others and to yourself."

At first, Arav nodded. He had come ready to surrender. But as the monk stood and approached him, hands rising to begin the ancient ritual, something within Arav stirred.

No. This wasn't right. This wasn't how it was supposed to end.

He took a step back. "There has to be another way! Train me again, guide me... I can change."

The monk shook his head. "It's too late, Arav. You've already tasted what shouldn't be consumed."

Arav's breath turned sharp. The sword at his side hummed faintly, almost in warning. "Don't do this... please."

"I must. For the good of all."

And with that, the monk began to chant the sacred words, the ones that would sever Arav's connection to the sword, to his strength, to his power.

But the fire inside Arav exploded.

In one swift motion, driven by desperation and the dark pride that had taken root in his soul, he drew Vyomdhara and slashed.

There was silence.

The monk staggered, his hands falling to his side. A red bloom spread across his robes, and his eyes—those wise, kind eyes looked at Arav one last time.

"You were meant to save... not fall," he whispered.

Then he collapsed beneath the Bodhi tree, his life fading like incense smoke.

Arav stood frozen, sword in hand, heart pounding. The weight of what he'd done began to crush him but it was too late. A new darkness surged through him. The moment the monk died, something deep and ancient awakened within the blade. A curse, buried in its core, now unshackled.

The sword pulsed with power, but not the kind Arav had once known. This was different. Malevolent. Hungry.

His breath grew heavy, his eyes darkened, and his skin felt hot like molten iron.

The fall was complete.

The protector had become the destroyer.

And the shadows welcomed him.

CHAPTER TWENTY

THE LAST LIGHT

Arav wandered the empty streets, the blood of his master still fresh on his blade and heavier on his soul. Neon lights flickered overhead, casting erratic shadows on the walls around him. Once he walked these streets as a hero; now every footstep echoed the silence of fear. Where once children cheered, now doors slammed shut at the sound of his presence.

His mind was a whirlwind of regret, confusion, and the cold void of guilt. He passed the same alley where he'd once saved a mother and her child. Now, even the air recoiled from him. The city, his home, rejected him.

He looked at his hands calloused, scarred, and now stained with the one sin he could never atone for. "What have I become?" he whispered.

His legs, as if guided by memory or fate, brought him to the edge of the forest. Beyond it, nestled in the ancient hills, stood the cave, the place where his journey began. The place where Vyomdhara had rested for a thousand years. The place where the light had once chosen him.

He entered slowly, his heart pounding not with fear, but with a desperate kind of hope. The monks who once protected the cave were gone, either dead or scattered by his fall. Only silence welcomed him now. The once-lit torches had turned to ash, the great stone doors creaked open with a ghostly moan.

He sat down before the pedestal where the sword once lay in slumber. The cave, dark and vast, echoed with every breath he took. He closed his eyes, forcing himself to remember everything.

He saw the boy who laughed with his friends, the one who didn't believe in fate. He saw the boy who found himself chosen, who wanted nothing but to protect. He remembered the thrill of his first battle, the warmth of camaraderie, the pride of victory.

He remembered the faces of those he helped, the silent thanks in their eyes. And then he remembered the shift, the thirst for justice becoming a hunger for control. The pride morphing into arrogance. The belief that he alone could determine right from wrong.

And he remembered the monk Parivrajaka his guide, his teacher, his only family. He saw his final breath. The pain in his fading eyes.

Tears fell freely now.

"I have lost everything... everyone," Arav whispered into the void. "All I ever wanted was to protect. And I became the very monster I swore to fight."

He looked at Vyomdhara. The once-glorious sword, now pulsing with a dull red hue, feeding off the darkness within him. The cave walls seemed to close in around him, pressing his guilt into every bone.

"I don't deserve this power," he muttered. "I don't deserve to live."

With trembling hands, he raised the sword. It felt heavier than it ever had before, as if it too resisted his decision. He knelt before the pedestal, bowed his head low, and aimed the blade at his chest.

"Let this end with me."

No voice came to stop him this time. No ancient warmth returned. There was only the wind that rustled through the cave, and the weight of his choice.

He closed his eyes.

With one deep breath, Arav drove the blade into his heart.

Time seemed to pause. The sword pierced through with a quiet finality. His body slumped forward, falling to the cold stone floor. His blood pooled beneath him—thick, dark, and silent.

Vyomdhara clattered beside him, its red hue dimming until it was extinguished.

As the last breath escaped his lips, the cave reacted. The torches flared once in bright blue, then faded to darkness. A wind circled the chamber, soft and mourning.

Arav's face, once twisted in torment, now looked calm. A faint smile tugged at his lips as though in death, he had found the peace life had denied him.

Outside, the first rays of dawn reached the mouth of the cave. Birds sang again, and the world turned as it always did. But deep in the earth, where light barely reached, a story ended.

A warrior had fallen.

A soul, burdened by power and pain, had chosen silence over fury.

And the sword, Vyomdhara, faded into legend once more.

The End.

A Note from the Author

To you — the reader who picked up The Invisible Sword and chose to stay till the very end — thank you from the bottom of my heart.

This story began as a simple idea in a quiet moment, and now it lives, because you gave it your time, your imagination, and your belief. Arnav's journey was never meant to be just about swords and demons it's about the unseen strength we all carry, the fire within us waiting to awaken.

Thank you for walking beside him, feeling his pain, cheering his growth, and trusting in the magic of destiny. I hope you saw a piece of yourself in him in his fears, his courage, and his quiet rebellion against being forgotten.

If this story made your heart race, your eyes tear up, or your spirit rise, then everything was worth it.

And remember: the invisible ones often have the loudest stories waiting to be told.

With all my love and gratitude,
VISHNU

-

About The Author

From the moment I first flipped through the pages of a fantasy novel or sat wide-eyed watching epic films unfold on screen, I knew stories were more than just entertainment — they were magic.

I've always been drawn to tales of lost heroes, ancient legends, and the quiet souls who rise to greatness. Writing The Invisible Sword was not just a creative journey, but a deeply personal one, a way to bring my love for mythology, fantasy, and storytelling to life.

I'm passionate about creating worlds where ordinary people discover extraordinary destinies where emotion meets action, and silence hides strength.

When I'm not writing, I'm usually buried in a book, watching films that stir the soul, or dreaming up the next story waiting to be told.

This is just the beginning and I hope you'll stay for the stories yet to come.

www.ingramcontent.com/pod-product-compliance
Lightning Source LLC
Chambersburg PA
CBHW021121130726
47988CB00003B/1101